SONOMA COUNTY LIBRARY

W9-BSD-638

WILLIS, JEANNE.
RELATIVITY, AS EXPLAINED
BY PROFESSOR XARGLE
1994.

10000624941904
GUER

SONOMA COUNTY LIBRARY

OFFICIAL
DISCARD

I

Professor Xargle

Text copyright © 1993 by Jeanne Willis
Illustrations copyright © 1993 by Tony Ross
All rights reserved.

CIP Data is available.

First published in the United States 1994 by
Dutton Children's Books,
a division of Penguin Books USA Inc.
375 Hudson Street, New York, New York 10014
Originally published in Great Britain 1993 by
Andersen Press Ltd., London
Printed in Italy by Grafiche AZ, Verona
First American Edition
1 3 5 7 9 10 8 6 4 2
ISBN 0-525-45245-1

RELATIVITY

AS EXPLAINED BY
Professor Xargle

Translated into Human by **JEANNE WILLIS**

Illustrated by **TONY ROSS**

DUTTON CHILDREN'S BOOKS ∗ NEW YORK

Good morning, class. Today we are going to learn
about Earth Families.

An Earth Family is a group of Earthlings that is
held together by relativity. This happens whether
the Earthlings like it or not.

Sometimes antique Earthlings are found in the same group as brand-new ones.

But the honkers and earflaps of each Earthling in
a Family always match.

Earth Families usually begin with one Daddy Earthling, one Mommy Earthling, and one Earthlet.

The number of relatives in an Earth Family is always larger than the number of chairs at the feeding table.

To show their affection, Brother and Sister Earthlets tap each other on the head with stuffed
objects.

Brother Earthlets are sticky and stinky and can be
dangerous. Never put your hand in their pockets.

Sometimes Brother Earthlets take wiggly worms
from their pockets and eat them for supper.

Sister Earthlets are sly and sneaky and can be rec-
ognized by their loud songs.

If you would like to hear one sing, drop a creepy with eight legs into her underfrillies.

When they are sad, Earthlets squirt gallons of
water from their eyes. This keeps them clean.

Here are Auntie and Uncle Earthling. When they come to visit, the Earthlets must frisk them for expensive presents.

Uncle Earthlings are also called Horsies.

This Earth Family is playing a game called "Be quiet. We are talking." The winner is the last one to fall asleep.

Here are some phrases I would like you to learn:

"Gosh, is that the time?"

"We really must be going."

Grandma and Grandpa Earthlings are also related
to Tyrannosaurus rex. They have been on Planet
Earth a long time.

Grandparent Earthlings are made from soft, crum-
ply material.

The Grandma Earthling can grow flowers and fruit
on her head.

At night, Grandma Earthling puts pink hedgehogs in her fur. Grandpa Earthling puts his chompers in a glass.

New and antique Earthlings like to play together. Here, a Family is having a contest to see who can throw the most bread without falling into the wet.

A popular Family game is called "Where did I put my glasses?" Everyone can play.

That is the end of today's lesson. Put on your disguises quickly. We have been invited to meet a very special Earth Family.

They live in a large house called a Palace and wear special headgear called Crowns. Do you all have your invitations?

Good. We will be landing in five seconds.